Beauty and the Beast

Illustr

D1410753

Troll

Beauty and the Beast:

Library of Congress Cataloging-in-Publication Data

Beauty and the beast.
    Beauty and the beast.

    SUMMARY: Through her great capacity to love,
a kind and beautiful maid releases a handsome
prince from the spell which has made him an ugly
beast.
    [1. Fairy tales.   2. Folklore—France]
I. Milone, Karen.
PZ8.B383Be   1981   398.2'1'0944   81-612
ISBN 0-89375-464-1
ISBN 0-8167-5277-X (pbk.)

This edition published in 2002.

Printed in the United States of America.

10 9 8 7

Beauty and the Beast

Once upon a time, there was a rich merchant who had three daughters. The youngest daughter was called Beauty, and this made her sisters very jealous. They were not as lovely as Beauty. They were not as generous and kind as Beauty. They were too busy thinking of themselves to be thoughtful of anyone else.

It so happened that misfortune befell the merchant. He lost everything he owned except a poor cottage in the country—so that is where he moved with his family. Beauty got up very early every morning and worked as hard as she could. She did the cooking, the cleaning, and the spinning. But her sisters slept late and did not lift a finger to help with the housework. Instead, they sat around feeling sorry for themselves.

One day, the merchant learned that one of his ships, which he thought had been lost, had finally come into port. If he went to meet the ship, perhaps he could save some of his fortune after all. So he asked his daughters what presents they would like him to bring back with him. The two oldest daughters asked him for new dresses and fancy shoes and pretty jewelry. But Beauty asked only for a rose, since she had not seen one in such a long time.

And so the merchant traveled to the port where his ship had docked. But when he got there, he found that he had been cheated. He was even poorer than when he had started out. There was nothing he could do but turn around and go home.

That night the weather grew bad, and it began to snow. Before long, the merchant was hopelessly lost in the forest. Suddenly, he saw a light shining through the trees. He followed it to a huge palace.

There seemed to be no one at home. But a fire was burning in the fireplace, and hot food had been set out on the table. So he entered the palace. As soon as the merchant had eaten, he fell fast asleep. In the morning, after breakfast, he looked around for his mysterious host, but he found no one.

He wandered out into the garden, where he saw a rose bush that reminded him of Beauty's request. He broke off a rose for her. Suddenly, he heard a strange noise, and turned to see a terrible beast.

"You ungrateful wretch!" roared the Beast. "I have treated you well, and now you steal my roses. For this, you must die!" The merchant fell to his knees and begged for mercy. He said that he had picked the rose for one of his three daughters. Upon hearing this, the Beast replied, "I will let you go if one of your daughters comes here to take your place. If none of them loves you enough to come here willingly, then you yourself must return within three months."

The merchant could not even think of asking his daughters to take his place. But he did want to see them again—even if he must leave them in three months. And so, he agreed.

When the merchant reached his cottage, he gave the rose to Beauty. "If you only knew what this rose has cost me," he said. Then he told his daughters about all that had happened and about his promise to the Beast.

"I will go in your place," announced Beauty. And although her father would not hear of it, Beauty would not change her mind. "You cannot stop me from following you back to the palace," she said. "I would rather be killed by the Beast than die of sorrow from losing you."

When three months had passed, Beauty and her father went to the Beast's palace. The Beast asked Beauty if she had come willingly, and Beauty replied that she had. "Good," said the Beast. "Then you may stay." And then he left the room.

The next morning, after her father had left, Beauty wandered through the palace. She discovered that all her needs were satisfied immediately. She found beautiful dresses and jewels in her room. Fine meals were prepared for her. And there were many books for her to read. She even found a magic mirror that she could look into whenever she wanted to see her father.

At dinner time, the Beast came to visit Beauty. "Do you really find me ugly?" he asked. And Beauty replied that she did. Then the Beast looked sad, and he left the room.

Each night, he came back to visit with her. But he was gentle and kind, and Beauty began to look forward to his visits. "It is a shame that he is so ugly," she thought, "for he is thoughtful and good." There was only one thing that Beauty did not like. Each night, the Beast asked her to marry him. And Beauty always replied, "No, Beast. I will not marry you."

One day, Beauty looked into her magic mirror and saw that her father was very ill. As soon as the Beast came to visit with her, she begged him to let her go. And the Beast replied, "You are free to go. But promise me you will return in eight days. For if you do not return, I shall die." When she had promised, he gave her a magic ring that would take her to her father's cottage and bring her back to the palace.

Beauty's father was overjoyed to see her, and he grew stronger every day. But when Beauty told her sisters how well she was treated at the Beast's palace, they were more jealous than ever. "She has no right to be happier than we are," they complained. "Perhaps if we trick her into staying here, the Beast will become so angry that he will kill her!"

So when it was time for Beauty to go, the sisters said, "You must stay longer. For if you leave now, our father will surely die." And so, Beauty agreed to stay. But only two nights later, she had a dream. She dreamed that the Beast was dying because she had broken her promise to him. As soon as she awoke, Beauty used the magic ring to take her back to the palace.

She found the Beast lying on a path in the garden. His
eyes were closed, and he was almost dead. Beauty ran to
him, crying, "You must not die, Beast! You must live, so
we can be married!"

Suddenly, the palace was brightly lighted, as if it had been decorated for a celebration. Beauty saw fireworks bursting all around the garden. And when she turned back to where the Beast had been, she saw a handsome prince. "Oh, where is my beloved Beast?" she cried.

"I was the Beast," replied the Prince. "But you have broken the enchantment and set me free by loving me in spite of my ugliness."

Beauty's father and sisters were invited to the palace for the wedding feast. But when her sisters saw how happy Beauty was, they became so jealous that they turned into stone statues. Beauty's father gave his blessings to his youngest daughter and the Prince. And they lived happily forever after.